GORKOH

Welcome to my BRILLIANT world.....

D0231207

Delia's sunglasses

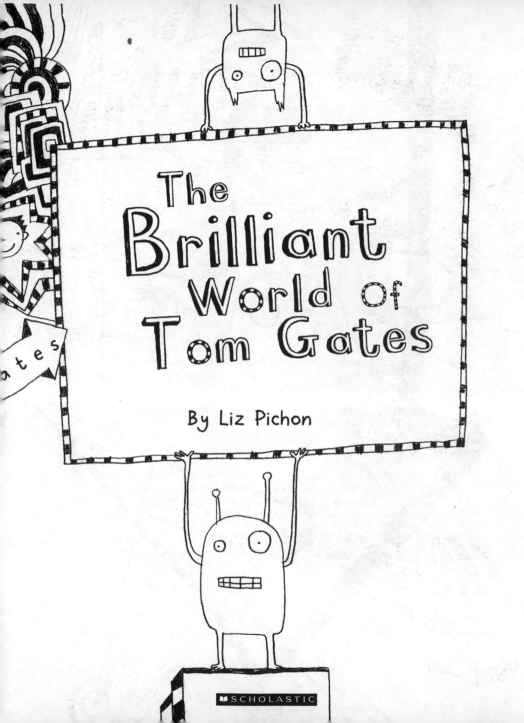

The Brilliant World of Tom Gates

By Liz Pichon

SCHOLASTIC

Published in the UK by Scholastic, 2021
Euston House, 24 Eversholt Street, London, NW1 1DB
Scholastic Ireland, 89E Lagan Road, Dublin Industrial Estate,
Glasnevin, Dublin, D11 HP5F

SCHOLASTIC and associated logos are trademarks
and/or registered trademarks of Scholastic Inc.

First published in the UK in 2011.

Text & illustration © Liz Pichon Ltd, 2011

The right of Liz Pichon to be identified
as the author and illustrator of this work has been asserted
by her under the Copyright, Designs and Patents Act 1988.

ISBN 978 1407 19343 4

A CIP catalogue record for this book is available
from the British Library.

Printed by CPI Group (UK) Ltd, Croydon, CR0 4YY
Paper made from wood grown in sustainable forests
and other controlled sources.

18

This is a work of fiction. Names, characters, places incidents and
dialogues are products of the author's imagination or are used
fictitiously. Any resemblance to actual people, living or
dead, events or locales is entirely coincidental.

www.scholastic.co.uk

Small
bug

This book **TOM GATES** is worth at

LEAST

10

MERITS !

IF not

More !

Dedicated to **LOADS** of lovely people

Mark

Zak ♥ Ella ♥ Lily

Thanks to Sarah S.
And to my dad, who really
did wear some
Seriously
embarrassing outfits.

strong bugs

ME ➩

YEAH!

①

Even though I only live four minutes away from my school, I'm often late.

This is usually because me and Derek (my best mate and next-door neighbour) "chat" a bit (OK, a LOT) on the way. Sometimes it's because we get distracted by delicious fruit chews and caramel wafers at the shop. Occasionally, it's because I've had loads of other very important things to do.

For instance, this is what I did this morning
(my first day back at school).

Woke up – listened to music
Played my guitar
Rolled out of bed (slowly)
Looked for socks
Looked for clothes
Played some more guitar
Realized I hadn't done my "holiday reading
homework"

PANICKED ⊙⊙ – thought of

good excuse for lack of homework (phew!).
Annoyed my sister, Delia. Which I admit did
take up a very LARGE chunk of the morning
(time well spent though).
Hid Delia's sunglasses.
Took my comic into the bathroom to read
(while Delia waited outside – Ha! Ha!). When
Mum shouts...

"Tom! You're LATE For School!"

Run past Delia (who's still waiting outside the bathroom and quite cross now). Ignore her sisterly love.

CREEP!

Save precious time by:

 Not brushing hair

Not brushing teeth (for very long)

 Not kissing Mum goodbye

(Too old for all that kind of thing.)

Eat the last piece of toast, then grab my packed lunch and my bike. Shout **BYE!** to anyone who can hear me.

Then bike to school in about two minutes flat.

Which is a **New** TOM GATES WORLD RECORD... And this is the REALLY good bit... **AMY PORTER** has just arrived too!

I am so pleased to see her after the holidays. I smile, in what I think is a nice friendly cheery way. ☺

Amy is not impressed. She looks at me like I'm weird (I'm not).

Me smiling

HI Amy!

(This is a bad start to my day.)
Then it gets worse...

Mr Fullerman (my form teacher) makes the whole class stand outside our room. He says

"Welcome BACK, Class 5F. I've got a BIG surprise for you ALL."

(Which is not good news.)

OH NO! He's rearranged ALL the desks! I'm now sitting right at the front of the class. Worse still, Marcus "Moany" Meldrew is next to me.

This is a DISASTER. How am I going to draw my pictures and read my comics? Sitting at the back of the class I could avoid the teacher's glares. I am SO close to Mr Fullerman now I can see up his nose.

Before

NOW

Front of the class

And if that's not bad enough, **M**arcus Meldrew IS the most annoying boy in the WHOLE school. He is **SO** nosy and thinks he knows everything.

Marcus Meldrew is already annoying me...

He is looking over my shoulder while I'm writing this.

He is **still** looking... ⊙ ⊙

Still looking...

Yes, MARCUS, I'm writing about

⟶ YOU ⟵

MARCUS MeLdrew

has a face like a mouse.

Marcus Meldrew has a face like a

Moose!

Moosy Marcus...

(He's stopped looking now.)

BUT on the other side of me, the good ☺ news is I am now sitting next to 👧 **AMY PORTER**, who is very smart and nice (even though she didn't seem thrilled to see me this morning).

BriLLIANT! At least I can have a sneaky look 👀 over her shoulder for a few right answers.

I think she is looking at me now.

AMY PORTER is <u>very</u> nice.

AMY PORTER is *SMART.*

She's not looking.

She's ignoring me ... I think.

So might as well stop writing nice things now
and draw a doodle instead.

(This cheers me up.)

Marcus
gets squished by a

BIG
Monster

11

Then **Mr F**ullerman says...

"As you can see, I've changed a few things around."

(Don't I know it!)

Then he begins to take the register.

(Usually I would take this opportunity to draw a few cool pictures, or take out my comic for a quick read. But I'm **SO** close to Mr Fullerman and his beady eyes, that I have to wait until he finishes and walks to the back of the class before I can get doodling in my book.)

OK, he's gone now. I'm thinking of names to call my band that Derek and I are in. We're not very good **YET**... but if I can think of a really good name, that will make us seem extra cool.

How about ALIEN TWINS? FOOT FIGHTERS?
I know ... DOGZOMBIES?

Mr Fullerman interrupts my drawing (I've turned the page over fast so he can't see it) and hands out the first piece of work we have to do this term. (Groan.)

Holiday Story Writing

Welcome back, Class 5F.

Today I would like you to write a story
about what you did on your summer holidays.

* Did you go away?
* Did you visit your family?
* What was the weather like and where did
  you stay?

Remember to describe everything in lots of
detail.

I am really looking forward to reading
all about your holidays!

Mr Fullerman

(My holiday wasn't a great success ...
but it does have a very happy ending.)

Here goes ⇨

Camping Sucks

This year Dad said, "Let's go camping, it's cheap." Mum didn't seem that keen, but I've never been camping before, so I was looking forward to it.

Dad and I went to the camping shop to buy a few essential items like:

"We won't need much," he said.

Dad

1. Tent
2. Sleeping bags
3. Cooking stuff
4. Fishing rods
5. ~~TV~~
6. ~~Computer~~

But the camping shop had some cool stuff and Dad got carried away. He spent a LOT of money and made me promise not to tell Mum.

"We could have stayed in a nice hotel, it would have been cheaper," Dad said.

"Not the same as sleeping under the stars and waking up in the fresh air!" said the man in the shop as he took Dad's money.

On top of everything Dad bought ... Mum packed a whole lot more. The car was stuffed. My sister, Delia, wasn't happy about coming with us. She's not allowed to stay in the house on her own any more, because she had a WILD party the last time Mum and Dad went away. (I stayed next door with Derek. His parents got woken up and weren't happy either.)

We set off, and for a while the holiday was going well. Then we took a wrong turning and got lost.

Mum blamed Dad for not listening to her properly. Dad blamed Mum for not reading the map the right way. They both blamed each other.

It was only when the car got a flat tyre that they stopped arguing. They phoned the Car Rescue Service, who eventually turned up.

It took **AGES** to fix the tyre and we didn't make it to the campsite until it was dark. Delia wasn't happy (Delia's never happy). She said the place looked **RANK** and she couldn't get a signal for her phone. Ha! ha! ha! I thought it looked OK. So I helped Dad with the tent while Mum unpacked the car. (Delia did nothing.)

The tent was tricky to put up, but we did the best we could.

It was a bit late to eat. Dad said, "I'll cook a big breakfast in the morning." But my stomach kept rumbling and I couldn't get to sleep. Then I remembered the secret stash of biscuits in my bag. So I grabbed them and ate them all! Crumbs got everywhere and it was very uncomfortable in my sleeping bag. Even though we had a "family tent" with separate rooms, Delia could hear me shifting around and fidgeting. It was really annoying her. BRILLIANT! So I did it some more. But at the same time I could also hear Mum and Dad ...

SNoring and that

was keeping me awake too. The noise was awful.
It seemed to be getting louder and LOUDER.
It was almost like thunder, deep and rumbly.
Then I realized it sounded like thunder ...
because it was thunder. Which was getting
closer. There was lightning, too, and
really heavy rain that was right
above our tent. The storm was
HUGE and it didn't take long for
the tent to blow away. AGH! HELP!

Everyone had to run to the car for
cover. The storm lasted all night long and
everything we had got wet and muddy.
Dad had pitched the tent RIGHT NEXT TO A
STREAM! Which flooded and all our stuff got
soaked.
Nobody slept at all. It was miserable.

Spot the
problem...

In the morning Dad tried to get his money back from the campsite owner (as we slept in the car).

He complained a lot, but it didn't work. Mum collected our soggy belongings, which were all ruined (including the tent). I could hear her muttering things like "Proper holiday next year" and "Greece" under her breath.

Delia was crying (again) because her mobile phone had got wet and wasn't working. That cheered me up. So I decided to try and make the best of the holiday and go exploring. There were lots of interesting-looking trees to climb. I was nearly at the **TOP** of one, when suddenly a branch SNAPPED under my foot.

I hadn't realized how high up I was until I fell down...

It was pretty
impressive, really...

Delia heard me YELP as I hit the ground.
She came over and just watched me as I rolled
around on the ground in pain holding my arm.
Ha! It felt REALLY BAD but Delia didn't
Ha! look too concerned.
Freak!

Eventually she got Mum.

"That's all I need," said Mum as she took me to the first aid tent. They gave me a lolly 🍭 and put my arm in a bandage (I was very brave). 🙂

It looked like our camping holiday was going to be very short. More rain was due so Mum and Dad decided under the circumstances (no tent or dry clothes) we should go home. 🙁

I wasn't that upset and Delia was delighted. So we all packed up and left the campsite. 🪧Home

On the way home we stopped off in a nice restaurant, where I managed to eat a huge pizza with my one good arm. My bad arm was really hurting 🙁 but I didn't complain because it was the first time in ages that everyone looked happy.

Our neighbours Mr and Mrs Fingle and Derek were surprised to see (·) (·) us back so soon. My bad arm was SO painful now that I went to my room to look at it.

Worryingly, it had turned purple and SWOLLEN up like a balloon. (·) (·)

I showed Mum and Dad. They looked shocked. Delia said "You look like a FREAK" (which was kind of her). Mum and Dad got back in the car and drove me to the hospital, leaving Delia at home.

Luckily ... my arm's not serious. I had just sprained it, and the bandage was put on too tight. So they redid it and put it in a very cool sling instead. (:)

(I'll live, apparently.)

It was quite late 🌙 by the time we got home and there was music BLASTING out from our house. Mum and Dad were FURIOUS

Delia had invited lots of her friends round for a party and BOY was she in trouble.

I forgot all about my sore arm because listening to Delia being told off and grounded by Mum and Dad was probably the → BEST PART

of my whole entire holiday.

What were you thinking?

You're grounded!

Yeah!

THE END

It sounds like you had a very
eventful time, Tom!
Excellent work. I felt like I was
there … but glad I wasn't!

5 Merits

WOW! Mr Fullerman liked my story!
I've never had **5** merits before.
I leave my book open so **AMY PORTER** can
see how clever I am. But she doesn't seem
too interested. Maybe this will help:

I got 5 MERITS

No, she's still not looking.

Marcus says he's got five merits as well.

"Great," I say.

"We're like twins now."

(He's so annoying.)

I show Mum and Dad my story because I think they'll be pleased with me (for a change).

Instead Mum gives me a note to give to Mr
Fullerman.

Dear Mr Fullerman

We are delighted Tom got five merits.
Also, can I just say that this is not the
usual type of holiday we have. We are
actually VERY responsible parents.

Tom's arm is fine now – in case you were
wondering (and in case he tries to get
out of doing PE).

Kind regards

Mr and Mrs Gates

I think Mum was worried my story made them
look bad.

BREAK time!

I am catching up with a few friends who I haven't seen over the holidays. Mark Clump got another pet (but he won't tell me what it is!).

Norman Watson's not allowed to eat sweets or ANYTHING with E-numbers in because they make him go really WILD. But I can see him running round the playground with his jumper over his head shouting, "I'm a space man, I'm a space man." Which makes me think he's had a few sneaky sweets already today.

Soloman Stewart (his nickname's SOLID) is the tallest boy in the whole school. He has GROWN even more, I think.

Then Derek comes over (he's in Mrs Worthington's class, not mine, because we chat too much). I've seen him loads during the holidays (his hair has grown — he hasn't).

I show him my ideas and drawings for a band name. (He likes DOGZOMBIES best ... me too.)

When Marcus Meldrew barges into our chat.

"What's that?"

"Ideas for our band."

"What band?"

"Me and Derek are in a band and we're thinking of what to call ourselves."

"That's easy."

"Really?" (Marcus has an idea.)

"Yeah... Just call yourselves

'The Total Losers'.

Ha! Ha! Ha!" says Marcus.

Who's even more annoying this year than he
was last year (if that's possible).

Marcus
being a
TWIT

Ha!

Ha!

Ha!

Homework already from Mr Fullerman.
(It's like we never had a holiday.)

HOMEWORK

I'd like you all to write a REVIEW.

It could be a review of a book,
play, concert or film: something you
have seen or read.

Ask yourself lots of questions:

Describe the film/book/concert.
What did you like or not like?
What was it about?

Looking forward to reading them very
much.

Mr Fullerman

(I'll see what's on telly tonight, then read the
newspaper review. That's always a good start.)

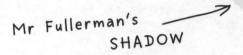

Mr Fullerman's
SHADOW

S itting so close to Mr Fullerman is already proving tricky for me.
Because I am being forced to ... **work.**
It's **EXHAUSTING!**

(Amy doesn't seem thrilled to be sitting next to me. Maybe if she sees me working, she'll think I'm smart?)
I will try and impress her.

She's just caught me sneaking a look at her work. I pretend to be drawing, but I've been rumbled.

I know ... I'll draw something FUNNY.
Mr Fullerman with hair...

(Amy still not impressed.)

After lessons, I meet Derek by the bike shed. Our bikes are very cool. Mine's covered in stickers and doodles. Derek's is a bit battered but *super* fast. There's a very odd-looking bike in the shed which catches our eye (not in a good way). It's covered in FUR and FLUFF with silly wobbly eyes and weird bits hanging from the handles.

"It looks like Marcus," Derek laughs.
"Or Norman Watson on sweets!" I say.
"Bet it belongs to a little new kid who
doesn't know any better!" says Derek.
"What kind of person would have a stupid-
looking bike like that?" I laugh.

Ha! Ha! Ha! Ha! We both laugh!

Ha! Ha! Ha! Ha!

But AMY PORTER is NOT laughing because it's
her bike.

TuT
"TuT

School caretaker Stan is
shaking his head and tutting in a
disapproving way (which is making
his keys jangle) because I have
upset Amy (AGAIN!). She calls me an
and takes her bike away. I say

IDIOT

"sorry" but Amy ignores me. (She ignored my
five merits too.)

It's been a terrible day.

I'm a turtle

On the way home, I see posters for my favourite band, **DUDE 3**, all over the town.
Even this doesn't cheer me up.
Derek does his best to make me laugh.
But all I can think about is Amy calling me an idiot (harsh) and Marcus calling us losers.

"Look on the bright side," Derek says.
But when I ask Derek what the bright side actually is ... he doesn't know.
"It's a saying."
Great.
I'll have to think of a way to make it up to Amy, which is not going to be easy.

Band practice with Derek tonight might not be so good because there's absolutely NOTHING that will cheer me up now.

Not a thing...

MUM'S BOUGHT,

CARAMEL WAFERS

Caramel Wafers

FANTASTIC!

Brilliant! MY FAVOURITE!

Hooray Hooray Hooray! Hooray!
Hooray Hooray Hooray! Hooray!

(I've suddenly cheered up.)

Derek and I eat two caramel wafers each and drink some squash. (Perfect preparation for band practice.)

Mum tells me to:

"Leave one for Delia!"

(As if!)

Instead, I take the last one and show Derek my favourite wafer/biscuit trick.
Which goes like this:

1. Remove wafer biscuit from wrapper really carefully.
2. Eat last wafer biscuit quickly before Delia comes home (half each).
3. Carefully re-fold wrapper to look like wafer is still inside. (empty)
4. Watch Delia open the empty wafer wrapper (ha ha).

M y trick worked a TREAT.

I can hear Delia moaning to Mum about me downstairs. So I take the opportunity to sneak into her room and borrow a few copies of **ROCK WEEKLY** for Derek and me to look at.

(Good inspiration for band practice. There are loads of good pictures of bands inside.)

W e take turns to try out a few

ROCK STAR POSES.

Delia's sunglasses

Some of them are more successful than others.

(Mustn't forget to do this week's homework — write a review... Should be easy.)

Mr Fullerman

I'm very <u>SORRY</u>.

You'll never guess what happened.

I had just finished writing my homework review when I accidentally spilt the **BIGGEST** glass of water all over it.

I am very upset, as it was a **VERY** good review. (Probably worth at least five merits, if not six.)

AGH!

Oh dear, Tom!

What a mess. I will look forward to seeing it redone for tomorrow. Watch out for those BIG pesky glasses of water in future!

Ho**m**e work

(I think I got away with that excuse, will definitely do it for tomorrow.)

Art

Art now ... brilliant, as it's one of my favourite lessons.

Mr Fullerman would like us all to draw a self-portrait.

These will be put up around the **WHOLE SCHOOL** for everyone to see (and laugh at, probably).

Mr Fullerman hands out small mirrors so we can look at ourselves while we're drawing (which is not easy at all).

The class are all concentrating and quiet for a change. Apart from Norman Watson, who keeps shining his mirror in other people's faces, so he's moved.

Then Mrs Worthington (Derek's teacher) comes in and takes over from Mr Fullerman, who goes off to do something more important (like drink coffee and read newspapers).

Mrs Worthington sometimes takes us for maths. She is always very enthusiastic about everything. She is being very enthusiastic now.

Hello! Hello! Lovely Class 5F!

"I'm looking forward to seeing all your lovely pictures," she tells us happily.

Because I like art and drawing, I'm working extra hard.

Amy's self-portrait looks a bit odd. (She doesn't really look like that at all.)

Hers is still better than Marcus's. He's drawn himself with a really BIG head (well, that bit's true to life).

Mrs Worthington sees I've finished my portrait and comes over to take a closer look.

"What a marvellous picture, Tom!" she says.

"Mr Fullerman will be pleased!" she adds.

But I'm not really listening to her ... because I have suddenly noticed that this close up, Mrs Worthington has something on her top lip that looks a bit like, well,

 like a ...

I am trying really hard not to stare.
(It's tricky not to.)

(Don't stare... Don't stare...
Look at her face, not her moustache.)

"Tom, why don't you do another
wonderful portrait?"

Good idea.

"Only this time, really think about
the person you're drawing. And don't forget to
put in *LOTS* of detail."

OK, Mrs Worthington,
I'll do my best.

Here goes...

I'm getting the feeling that Mrs Worthington doesn't like my portrait very much (or me) now.

Oakfield School
Re: Tom Gates

Dear Mr and Mrs Gates

I'm very sorry to inform you that Tom has a detention tomorrow lunchtime. This is due to an unfortunate portrait he drew of me. I do hope Tom will learn the lesson that there is a BIG difference between drawing a portrait with detail ... and just being rude.

Yours sincerely

Mrs Worthington

(Lesson learnt. Don't let teachers see my drawings in future.)

When I get home, Dad ALREADY knows about my detention because Mrs Worthington has phoned. And more bad news — Delia took the phone call so she knows about it too.

GREAT, like the letter wasn't enough. Mrs Worthington might as well have announced my detention with a plane

TOM has Detention!

or a hot air balloon

TOM HAS DETENTION

so everyone in the whole town knows... (Groan.)

Dad tells Mum and now Derek isn't allowed to come round for band practice tonight. AND she's making me do an extra chore.

"Sweep the kitchen floor or take out the bins" (which smell). Some choice.

Delia is LOVING this. She keeps saying

"Diddums" to me in a really

stupid baby voice which is driving

me crazy. (But I can't let her see

she is getting to me, or

she'll keep on saying it **ALL** night

long, and probably tomorrow and the

next day too.)

Dad gives me one of his little (chats)

and tells me if I don't work hard at school,

I'll end up like him. Not such a bad thing if

you ask me, because Dad's

got a pretty good job.

Chat
Chat

He has his own office (well, it's a shed in our garden) where he works on his computer designing stuff. Occasionally he gets to work in other people's offices.

Mum likes it when that happens because he has to look smarter and he earns more money.

I prefer it when Dad works at home because he has a SECRET stash of caramel wafers in the shed that I eat (and Mum doesn't know about).

So there I am sweeping the kitchen floor when Granny Mavis pops over to borrow a cookbook.

Hello, Tom! Just popping by to pick up a cookbook!

(I call my granny and granddad

because they
are both old
and very ancient.)

"You never use cookbooks!" Mum says in a
surprised way.

"I'm inviting the whole family round for
lunch," Granny says.

"Really?"

(Oh dear ... that's not really 🙁 very good
news. Let me explain...)

Granny Mavis and Granddad Bob are not your usual kind of grandparents.

Especially when it comes to meals. They like to experiment and eat very odd combinations of food.

pear onion soup

tea ON cornflakes

(Saves time apparently.)

(More on that later.)

Also, Granny is just RUBBISH at cooking. So Mum loads her up with a pile of cookbooks in the hope she might actually follow a real recipe.

I'm still sweeping and trying to make Granny feel sorry for me by doing my "sad face". Hopefully she'll slip me a bit of extra pocket money (Granny does that sometimes).

But Mum tells Granny [why] I'm sweeping the kitchen.

Oh dear...

Rude drawing!

("Detention ... blah blah ... drawing ... blah blah ... moustache ... blah blah.")

And *now* she wants me to go to the shop to buy Milk! (work work work) "So Granny can have a cup of tea."

Luckily Granny gives me extra money to buy myself a treat.

RESULT

In the shop, I'm deciding how to spend my treat money (sweets? caramel wafers?) when I spot ⊙ ⊙ this month's copy of

ROCK WEEKLY

And on the cover is the best band in the whole world. **DUDE 3**

I **HAVE** to buy it! And there's even enough money left for two fruit chews as well. **BRILLIANT!**

Mum asks, Where's the milk?

(Suddenly I remember why I went to the shop and hide my copy of **ROCK WEEKLY**.)

"The shop had run out," I say.

(*PHEW!* Quick thinking ... must tell Derek about **DUDE 3**.)

Granny Mavis has hot water with a slice of carrot instead which is a bit bonkers even for her.

Odd

I have read the whole interview with **DUDE3**.
And I can't believe that they are actually coming
to play a concert *IN* OUR TOWN.

I go on the computer to listen to their
latest tracks and see where else they're
playing.✳

This is AMAZING. Derek is online
and is just as excited about it as I am.

**Dude3 Dude3 Dude3! WHOOOOOO
HOOOOOOO!!**

**Can't wait, DUDE MAN. Will SO be
there!!!**

**ME TOO ... BRILLIANT!! Can I read
your mag after? Bring to skool yeh!**

**Spread the DUDE3 word.
Dad calling, time for burnt food.**

**Pretend it's fast food ...
and eat it really fast... LOL!**

**Ha! Ha! Give it to Delia ... she won't
see it with her dark glasses. FREAK!**

✳www.dude3.com

Good news about the concert. **B**ad news — me and Derek are too young to go on our own. Dad will probably want to come too. Which is OK as long as I can get him to **PROMISE** not to:

1. Sing

2. Dance

3. Wear anything embarrassing

Which could be tricky because he likes to do all those things (sometimes at the same time).

I did it MY way

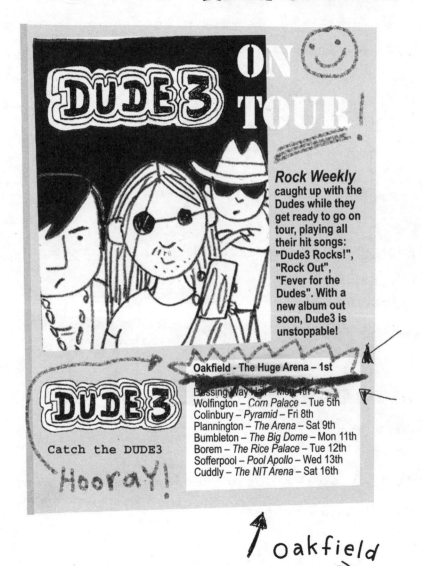

Hardly slept at all last night. ☺, ☺

All I can think about is that

are coming to town. FANTASTIC.

Even Delia seems excited. (For her, anyway ...
it's hard to tell.)

As long as she doesn't stand anywhere near
me, I'm not bothered.

The tickets cost a LOT of money.
If I'm going to get DAD to pay for them,
I will have to be on [best] behaviour at all
times. This will be tough but worth it.

I'm reading my copy of **ROCK WEEKLY** in the bathroom while Delia is ¡BANGING¡ on the door outside. The crosser she gets, the slower I read, and brushing my teeth takes **AGES.**

It makes me late for school again (worth it, though). So I don't bother brushing my hair, just grab my clothes off the floor to wear (they're crumpled ... but who cares).

clothes pile

Then I stuff as much toast in my mouth as possible and take an apple to eat on the way (which is not easy on a bike).

Toast

I make it to Mr Fullerman's class with **30** seconds to spare.

Me being busy...

I'm feeling pretty pleased with myself, so I try another cheery smile at Amy, who for some reason makes a "YOU'RE DISGUSTING" face at me.
Why?

Me Smiling

Hi Amy!

Mr Fullerman announces,

"I hope you've all remembered it's your Individual School Photo today."

NO! NO! NO!

(I forgot.)

Smug mug Marcus obviously did remember. He's
looking all shiny neat and new. Ugh.

I'm looking slightly more crumpled than usual
due to my rushed start to the day. Oh well,
never mind. How bad can a school photo be?

The whole class line up in the hall. I'm second in line after Norman Watson, who is all twitchy and jumpy. (I really hope Norman's not

eaten any sweets.)

The photographer asks Norman to
"stop jiggling around."

(Oh dear ... he's definitely had sweets.)

Eventually (after LOADS more goes) Norman sits still just long enough for one photo to be taken.

The photographer whispers,

"This is going to be a very long day."

Then it's my turn.

Florence Mitchell (another super-smart girl) and Amy are watching me along with the rest of the class.

I have an idea. I will try and look and all MEAN and MOODY, a bit like the photos of DUDE3 in ROCK WEEKLY.

BRILLIANT!

But the photographer is not impressed and tells me to "CHEER UP!"

So I try and smile (a bit) ... then he says REALLY LOUDLY:

"Oh dear, you've got something NASTY stuck between your teeth."

(SHAME!)

He walks over and hands me a mirror. (Could this be any more embarrassing?)

"Better do something with your messy hair too – here's a comb."

Now EVERYONE is looking at me.

(It just got a lot more embarrassing.)

I have toast crumbs round my mouth and bits of apple skin stuck between my teeth. (Why didn't Amy <u>tell</u> me?) And now I've gone bright red too.

So much for a cool school photo. It's going to be hideous. 🙁

The photographer takes my picture and I can't get out of the hall fast enough. I have humiliated myself in front of the

ENTIRE class.

Now I will be forced to hide this school photo from everyone for the rest of my life. Especially Mum. She likes to send my school photos to <u>all</u> relatives across the

WHOLE WIDE WORLD.

TOM'S School Photo

There are second cousins in Outer Mongolia who have my school photos on their walls.

To Vera Gates
5 Green Lane
Outer Mongolia
The World
(Tom GATES photo enclosed)

BREAK TIME

I'm looking for Derek in the playground and I can't find him anywhere. His bike is in the shed, so I know he's here. I wonder if his school photo was as bad as mine? (Impossible.)

I ask Soloman "Solid" Stewart (the TALLEST boy in the whole school) if he can see him.

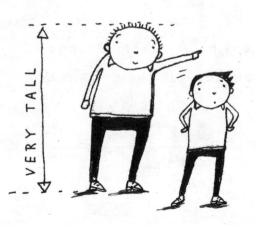

VERY TALL

Solid points to a boy on the climbing frame.
He looks a bit like Derek, but it can't be him
because his top button is done up AND he's
got a horrible neat side parting.

SIDE
PARTING

"Mum made me," Derek says. "For the school
photo." (Shame.)

Then Derek hangs upside down on the climbing
frame and his hair goes back
to normal. Which is just as
well, because no one in

DOGZOMBIES should
ever have a neat side parting
like that.

More importantly, Derek and I chat about...

1. How **DUDE3** are the **BEST** band ever.

2. How we REALLY <u>need</u> to go and see them.

3. How **DOG ZOMBIES** need to practise more to become the **BEST** band **EVER**.

4. **BISCUITS** – which are better, chocolate HobNobs or caramel wafers?

5. Which biscuits to eat at band practice.

Chocolate **or** caramel?

CARAMEL WAFERS

Who cares about stupid school photos?

Maths

Mr Fullerman hands out our maths worksheets.

On the outside I'm forcing myself to look fascinated and interested in Mr Fullerman's sums. When really on the inside I am still reliving the humiliation that was my school photo, over and over and over again.

HIDEOUS School Photo

I wish it was the end of school right now. So to cheer myself up, I draw a few more band logos and ideas.

I'm careful to do some sums as well so it looks like I'm "working out" my answers.

A dog what's a zombie

Which one?

24 +
32
56

DOG ZOMBIES

DOG ZOMBIES

DOG ZOMBIES

10 +
10
20 ← I am a Genius!

Marcus is straining his head and trying to look over my shoulder so he can see ⊙⊙ what I'm doing.

GET LOST, MARCUS...

Marcus + Marcus = IDIOT

Mr Fullerman is looking at me now. So I put my arm right over my drawings and do a few more sums.

Marcus is LEANING back in his chair now to see over my arm. I think he can see my doodles, so I turn my back on him. And he leans FORWARD. Then I LEAN back, and he puts his head on the table as if he's trying to see under my arm. Ha!

"MARCUS ... stop trying to look at Tom's work and concentrate on your own!"

Yes, Marcus. NO cheating. Serves him right.

Then while the attention is on Marcus, I take the chance to have a sneaky glance at ◯◯ Amy's sums and memorize a few answers. (At least this way I will definitely get some sums right.)

Then I carry on with my drawings. (I'll show them to Derek later.) This maths lesson is turning out to be quite good after all.

RESULT! ☺

Mr KEEN is Oakfield School's headmaster. He likes to "POP" into classes to see what we're up to.

Today he decides to say hello to Class 5F (us). Luckily I have some impressive-looking maths in front of me. (Thanks mostly to Amy.)

"Hello, Class 5F."

"Hello, Mr Keen."

Mr Keen then launches into the usual type of headmaster "chat".

While he does that, here are a few interesting

FACTS about Mr Keen.

over

1. He has a very RED face that gets redder when he gets cross.

2. Mr Keen gets cross quite easily.

Here's a RED-O-METER that shows clearly the different stages of redness Mr Keen's face goes through.

ANGRY
Very Angry
CROSS
RAGING
RED-O-METER

3. Mr Keen's eyebrows look like two HAIRY Caterpillars crawling across his face.

Mr Keen is still chatting when my stomach starts to make really LOUD grumbly hungry noises (it's nearly lunchtime). I'm hoping he might take the hint and stop talking. But he carries on.

When my stomach growls again I pretend it's not me by staring at Marcus.

The bell goes off for lunch but Mr Keen still keeps rambling on and on.

"I'll let you all go to lunch now," he says.

(ABOUT TIME.)

There's a trick to rushing down to the dinner hall without looking like you're **PUSHING** anyone out of the way. Very fast walking does the trick.

Fast walking

I grab my lunch box and try not to take in the smell of the

U.F.O.S

(Unidentified Food Objects)

that are being served up.

On Mondays, Tuesdays and Wednesdays I have packed lunch. On Thursdays and Fridays I have school dinners.

This is because on Thursdays **AMY PORTER** has school dinners and on Fridays it's CHIPS.

Derek is already sitting at the table eating. So I sit next to him, and then Norman Watson sits next to me. When I open my lunch box there's a note inside from my Granny Mavis.

Enjoy!
Love
Granny
xx

(**Oh NO!** I forgot. Granny likes to help out and make my packed lunch when she visits. And I wasn't there to stop her.)

La!
La!
La!

I'm really hoping that she hasn't actually tried to cook **anything** odd for me.

Looking 👀 in my lunch box, I can see something that looks a bit like a pizza.
It is a pizza.
(So far so good.)

Made in the shape of a face.
I think?

It's *my* face ... groan.

On the pizza there's

cheese (OK)

tomatoes (OK)

olives (UGH).

And something else that I personally don't think should EVER in a

million years be seen on a pizza ... ever ...

La!
La!
La!

(What was Granny thinking?)

A BANANA!

There's a banana on my pizza.
I take it off really quickly before anyone sees
that I have a banana on my pizza and thinks
I'm weird.
Too late...
Amy and Florence walk past me and both pull
a "that's disgusting" face at me and sit at
another table.
Then Norman Watson nudges me and says,

"Is that a banana on your pizza?"

"Maybe..." I say.

"**YUM!** I'll have it if you don't want it."

So I let Norman eat my banana and don't ask any questions. Derek whispers, "That's gross" to me. But Norman seems happy enough, so I keep quiet. I eat the rest of the pizza anyway. (It tastes a bit banana-ish in places.)

Granny Mavis has a few more unusual surprises for me lurking in my lunch box:

Cucumber juice in a can.

Lavender and potato biscuits.

And a lemon. (Why?)

Derek has some more normal food for lunch, which he shares with me. (That's why he's my best mate.)

Best mate

We're just about to go out to break when Mrs Mumble (that's her real name) makes an announcement over the tannoy system. No one can ever understand what Mrs Mumble says, so you have to listen carefully.

"Hello! Will Tom Gates come to see Mrs Worthington... Tom Gates..... Thank you!

I think she said Tom Gates to see Mrs
Worthington? ... She did.
I forgot about my detention.

GROAN.

I have to help Mrs Worthington put up all
the portraits we did.
(Not the one I did of her, obviously.)

When she's not looking I add a few extra
details to Marcus's portrait.

Which I think are a great improvement.

CLASS 5F SELF-PORTRAITS

Ross White

Paul Jolly

Soloman Stewart

Julia Morton

Norman Watson

Pansy Bennet

Mark Clump

Amber Tulley Green

Amy Porter

Trevor Peters

Brad Galloway

Leroy Lewis

Tom Gates

Florence Mitchell

Indrani Hindle

Marcus Meldrew

OH NO, Mr Fullerman's been

looking in my book.

> Tom
> I'm sure DOGZOMBIES is a fantastic band.
> But you need to concentrate on your
> MATHS in future. (By the way, I like
> this logo best.)

Mr Fullerman

I make a huge effort to pay attention in
lessons, as I can't afford to get into any
more trouble. Especially if I want Dad to buy
DUDE3 tickets.

Even though I know that Mum and Dad will now use this at every opportunity to make me do stuff that I really don't want to do, like:

"Eat your vegetables ... if you want those **DUDE 3** tickets."

"Tidy your room ... if you want those **DUDE 3** tickets."

"Let your sister in the bathroom first ... if you want those **DUDE 3** tickets."

I can hear them now. Blah Blah! Blah Blah!

This is not going to be easy.

I'm trying to be extra good in Mr Fullerman's lesson.

I even volunteer to hand out the school trip forms.

Marcus tries to grab his form from me straightaway.

I say "Manners" to him, then leave him until last. Making him reach for his form a few times is fun. Until Mr Fullerman gives me one of his SCARY glares.

Teacher STARE

The trip actually looks like it could be quite good.

Year 5 class trip to the British Museum to look at **the Egyptians and mummies**.

Dear Parent/Carer

This term we will be studying the Egyptians and would like to take all the classes to the British Museum as part of the project.

This will be for the whole day and the children will need a packed lunch. We will be travelling by coach and we will need helpers on the day if anyone is available.

Please fill in the form below, which gives your child permission to attend the trip.

Many thanks

Mr Fullerman

Tear off and return to school **ASAP**.

Child's Name **Tom Gates** Class ___5F___

I give permission for my child to go to the British Museum
(YES)/NO ☺   ___Rita Gates___ Print___Rita Gates___

Signed___Rita Gates___   (good job!)

Does your child have any allergies? **Yes**
If so, what are they?___Do not give Tom ANY vegetables___
Are they taking any medicines? If so, what?___Yes... cough sweets. Or just SWEETS would be fine___

Are you able to help on the trip?___No NoNo___
Contact name ~~~~~~~~~
Contact number ~~~~~~~~~

(All done.)

Today Mr Fullerman asks us to read out
to the class our "What we did on holiday"
stories. I feel happy about this because I got

 merits for mine.

It will be a good opportunity to impress Amy,
hopefully.

Norman Watson reads his first.

He went to DISNEYLAND.
He's SO lucky! (But he didn't get five merits
like me. Ha!)

Marcus Meldrew got sent away to summer
camp for nearly the WHOLE HOLIDAY.
I think he annoys his parents as
much as he annoys me. (I'd send
him away for the whole year if I could.)

Julia Morton's "I found an interesting shell" story is not interesting at all.

This lesson is starting to get a bit dull when Mark Clump stands up and reads "MY NEW PET SNAKE", which gets my attention.

He tells us about the mice he keeps in the freezer to feed the snake with.

And how he bought the snake, where it lives, what the snake is called (Snakey ... not very original). It's a really good holiday story.

And the BEST bit about the whole story is when he reaches inside his desk and brings out...............

It's awesome. But Mr Fullerman doesn't think so. Neither do half the class, who run out. SCREAMING

M r Fullerman makes Mark put his snake away. The school office ring his mum, who comes to pick them both up. Which is a shame, because I really like snakes and I didn't get to see it properly.

At the end of school we get a note to take home.

Dear Parent/Carer

Please can we remind all children and parents that NO PETS of any kind can be brought into school.

Pets are for home, not for the classroom. Especially pets that can be considered slightly scary (like snakes).

Thank you

Mr Keen
Headmaster

Talking of pets, Derek is getting a new pet DOG. I can't wait! Delia is allergic to dogs so I'm not allowed to get one. But Derek can bring his dog round ALL the time because:

1. I really like dogs.

2. Delia will be forced to stay in her room or she'll have to go out. Either way she won't be around to annoy me.

Perfect!

Derek's Dog

Derek sends me a photo of his dog...

This weekend the whole family are having lunch at the old **FOSSILS'** house.

Mum is stressed about what we'll be eating, especially since I mentioned my banana pizza.

Dad is stressed because his brother (my Uncle Kevin) and his family will be there. Uncle Kevin seems to know a lot of things. Dad says it's because he's a "know-it-all".

Aunty **A**lice always laughs at Uncle Kevin's jokes, even when they're not funny (which is most of the time).

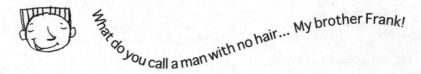

What do you call a man with no hair... My brother Frank!

Ha Ha! Ha!

Delia is in a bad mood because she doesn't want to go. I say, "Delia's got a boyfriend, Delia's got a boyfriend," which puts her in an even WORSE mood.

Mum and Dad say she HAS to come.

Something tells me this lunch isn't going to be much fun.

Luckily the Fossils are in a VERY good mood and happy to see everyone, which helps a lot.

Yo! kids!

Hello!

My twin cousins are already there (and eating ... they eat loads). They are even taller than Solid. I say "Hi" to them. They don't talk much; they just wave at me.

Mum asks what we're eating for lunch today. We all listen nervously.

Granny announces we're having:

Chicken stuffed with cheese.

Roasted eggs?

Peas on a stick.

I really hope it tastes better than it sounds.

We're all sitting at the table when Uncle Kevin asks Dad if he's got balder, which makes Aunty Alice laugh.

Ha Ha!

Dad doesn't look too happy.

Granny steps in and asks,

"Is everything OK?"

We all say, "Yes!"

"Delicious!" "Mmmmm!"

And nice things like that. But I notice no one is eating very much apart from the cousins. And Delia is secretly texting under the table.

Uncle Kevin starts talking about their

"AMAZING three-week holiday in Greece".

So I tell everyone about our terrible two-day camping holiday and how it rained and the tent was washed away because Dad STUPIDLY put the tent up by the stream. And then how I fell out of the tree...

Aunty Alice and Uncle Kevin seem to be enjoying the story.

Ha Ha!   Ha Ha!

Mum and Dad are GLARING at me in a "BE QUIET" kind of way.

Granddad changes the subject and asks me about my band.

So I tell him about **DOGZOMBIES** and then I tell everyone that **DUDE3** are coming to play in our town!

"Dad is SO brilliant, he's promised to buy tickets for us to see them," I say.
(Dad looks surprised but doesn't say no.)

I'm a genius.

BEST DAD

Turns out that the cousins are HUGE fans of **DUDE3** too. It's the most excited I've seen them since they won a chocolate fountain at their school fair.

Uncle Kevin suggests we all go together on a "big family night out". I don't mind who I go with as long as it's not just Delia. So I say "GREAT!" But Dad doesn't look pleased at all with the idea. Especially when Uncle Kevin starts going on about Dad's "terrible taste in music when we were growing up".

Dad is just about to say something to Uncle Kevin when Granny bursts into the room with...

"PUDDING!"

She has to explain what pudding is, because no one can tell.
It's a MASSIVE pile of bright pink pancakes that taste OK but look like horrid raw bits of liver.

On the way home, we stop off for fish and chips because everyone is still hungry.

Mum and Dad don't seem happy.

Delia is miserable (no change there then).

But I am VERY happy because:

1. I'm definitely going to see **DUDE3** now.

2. Granny gave me some sweets and a pound on the way out.

RESULT! Can't WAIT to tell Derek.

(All I have to do now is ask **Amy** to the concert.)

Today I was only a tiny bit late for school. Hiding Delia's sunglasses took slightly longer than usual. Slipping them into an open bag of salad was inspired, I thought. Delia would NEVER have found them if Mum hadn't been making sandwiches.

I got out of the house before Delia or Mum got the chance to tell me off.

Just crept into class in time for registration.

Mr Fullerman looks up from the register and asks me why I'm late. I do what anyone would do in my position. Blame my older sister for locking me in the bathroom.

Mr Fullerman makes a note of my excuse in the register, then moves on.

PHEW!

AMY PORTER isn't in the slightest bit interested in my excuses because she is too busy memorizing her

SPELLINGS!

(OH! NO! NOT the spelling test.)
This is <u>not</u> a good start to the day. I'm panicking and wondering how I'm going to get through this when something brilliant happens. I look over at Mr Fullerman's desk and I *think* I can see all the answers to this week's spellings test. The paper is turned over, but I can make out what the words are backwards. And copy them down quickly before anyone notices.

Like this.

(This test will be easy-peasy now!)

(What I can see.)

Bananas
Areas
Cameras
Radios
Umbrellas
Piano
Solo
Fiesta
Plastic

(What I write down.)

Bananas
Areas
Cameras
Radios
Umbrellas
Piano
Solo
Fiesta
Plastic

Mr Fullerman begins the test. I'm pretending to think carefully and write them down. And straightaway I realize there's a very BIG problem.

These spellings are not the same as Mr Fullerman's. Which makes me think I've written down next week's test instead.

I'm panicking, my mind's gone blank and I've missed the first **THREE** spellings already.

FOUR spellings ... FIVE spellings ... SIX-SEVEN-EIGHT ... the whole test. I keep pretending to write so Mr Fullerman doesn't suspect anything and hope for the best. **If** Mr Fullerman spots that I already have next week's test, he might smell a rat!

cheat

The test is over and we have to swap papers with the person next to us so they can mark them. Marcus hands me his paper.
Oh dear, I'm in trouble now..

I have to think quickly...

AGH!

Disaster has struck in the shape of a leaking pen.

Mr Fullerman makes me clean up my ink "accident". WHOOPS!

I get to check Marcus's test.
He thinks he's done very well and is looking extra smug.

Marcus Meldrew

1. potaoe ☹ ✗
2. Volcano ✓
3. Tattwo ☹ ✗
4. Kangeroow ✗
5. Hero ✓
6. Igloow ✗
7. Echo ✓
8. Mangoe ✗ $\frac{3}{8}$

Only 3/8 for Marcus.

Not so smug now.

Amy got 8/8 (she's so smart).

I say " WOW! Well done, Amy" (it's winding
Marcus up).
"You're SO good at spelling, aren't you?"
Then Amy says, "Thanks ... but I can't draw
like you can" (she actually said something nice
to me).

So while the class are checking spellings I
show Amy my latest **DOGZOMBIE**
drawings and ask her to pick the best one.
(She chooses the same one as Mr Fullerman.)

This is the longest conversation I have ever had with Amy. I tell her about **DUDE 3** and how they're playing in our town.

And it turns out that **A**my REALLY likes them too, which is **BRILLIANT!**

I'm trying to think about the best way to invite Amy to see **DUDE 3** when she says she likes singing.

I say, "I like singing too," then she says "Really?" and I say,

"**YES,** I can't get enough of singing."
So she suggests I join the school choir (like her) and I hear myself say,
"That's a **great** idea, I'd **LOVE** to join the choir."

(WHY? WHY? WHY did I say that?**)**

Which is exactly what Derek says when I tell him,

     "I'm joining the choir. It will be good for my singing and the band."

"You think so?" (Derek is not convinced.)

(No, I don't think so. But I'm hoping Amy will come and see DUDE 3 and I can't tell Derek that.)

I pass a choir practice poster on the school notice board. And I can't believe rehearsals are at LUNCHTIME! I don't even get to miss a boring lesson or two.
I'll go maybe once or twice to keep Amy happy - then drop out later on.

Good plan.

School Assembly

It's a "special assembly" today.

I can't believe that MARCUS is getting an award for his holiday homework! This seems very unfair as I got 5 merits as well.

Mr Keen, our headmaster, gives out prizes in front of the whole school.

It will be sick -making to watch Marcus being ultra smug. To make it worse, Mr Fullerman asks Marcus to take the register to the school office. Marcus thinks he's something special.

(While he's out of the class, I decide to add my own comments to his work.)

Smug

Mr Keen is standing in front of the whole school.

He is telling us the usual sort of things that headmasters like to say.

"Lots of hard work..." "Looking forward to..." Blah Blah Blah

I'm sitting behind SOLID,

so I can't see much of what's going on.

Mrs Nap leads the school in a rendition of "Morning Has Broken".
She is another one of those very enthusiastic teachers who *SWAYS* a lot from side to side while singing at the top of her voice.

Morning has BROKEN!

P_{ansy} B_{ennet} (don't mess with Pansy, she's tough) and of course Marcus are both getting awards.

B_{rad} G_{alloway} (who has cool hair) is next to me. I tell him to keep his eyes peeled on Marcus.

"Sssshhhhhhh."

Mr Fullerman is giving me the beady eye now.

BEADY eyes

M_r K_{een} says,

"Today we have some very important prizes to give out. Will Treasure Alexander and Grace Cole come up and get their certificates for good work on their shared nature project."

We all clap while the girls show everyone their impressive project.

"Will Pansy Bennet and Marcus Meldrew come up with their excellent 'My Holiday' homework."

Pansy holds her book up. It has some nice-looking writing and drawings in it. Everyone claps. Then she takes her certificate.
Next Marcus holds his work up to show the school. He's parading it around so the whole school can see what's written in his book.

Everyone bursts out laughing. And they keep laughing.

MY Holiday

I Am an IDIOT

Ha! Ha! Ha! Ha! Ha! Ha! Ha! Ha! Ha! Ha! Ha! Ha! Ha! Ha! Ha! Ha! Ha! Ha! Ha!

(I enjoy the moment.)

Marcus takes a certificate and sits back down quickly. He's still wondering why everyone was laughing at him.

I wish all assemblies were this much fun. Because for a short time, I forget all about promising to join the choir. It's only when assembly's over and I walk past that poster again that it all comes flooding back to me...

Groan.

cross

Mr Fullerman is not in a good mood now either. (He suspects I had something to do with "adding" to Marcus's work.)

He reminds me about my review and tells us about the school concert (the choir will be singing, apparently).

And if that's not enough, he gives us a parents' evening slip.

How am I supposed to fit in band practice now?

I manage to get through the rest of the lesson by concentrating VERY hard on two things.

1. What I'm going to eat for lunch.

2. The small black fly trying to land on Mr Fullerman's round head.

It takes a while, but the fly gets there in the end. And Mr Fullerman says,

"Glad to see you're paying such close attention to me, Tom."

Which makes me laugh. Then Amy mentions "choir practice this lunchtime".

"Great," I say. "Can't wait."

(groan.)

Mrs **N**ap welcomes the new faces (me) to the choir. I never knew **SOLID** was in the choir (he kept that quiet) and OH **NO**... Marcus is here too - great, I can't get away from him.

Amy looks pleased to see me, so that's something.

Mrs **N**ap puts me right next to Marcus

AGAIN.

She begins by making us do ridiculous warm-up exercises for our voices. We pull lots of silly faces and make odd noises. Then we learn the songs for the concert. Which is surprisingly fun. I'm *almost* starting to enjoy myself.

Mrs Nap asks us all to sway from side to side when we're singing.

We're supposed to all sway together in the same direction. But Marcus keeps swaying (accidentally on purpose) into me. So I *Sway* into HIM.

Then he SWAYS into me and *stamps* on my foot. So I give him a BIG *shove* (which gets him off my foot).

Then he SWAYS into me AGAIN so I *sway* just that little bit too HARD into him. And Marcus goes flying on to the floor (as if he's been hit by an elephant!).

N ow he's snivelling on the ground, shouting,

"Tom PUSHED ME.
TOM PUSHED ME!"
(He's SO annoying.)

Mrs Nap helps Marcus up. Then sends ME out, saying,

"**You** should know better, **Tom**. Perhaps choir is **not** for you after all."

I thought I was doing **SO** well.

I draw a picture of Marcus, which makes me feel better.

Marcus is a slimy toad.

CROAK!

HISTORY

Back in class, Marcus is sitting as far away from me as possible. (Just as well, I say.)

"Marcus is an idiot," Amy tells me. She saw him push me and tread on my foot. (Maybe choir practice was a good idea after all?)

While Amy is feeling a tiny bit sorry for me, I take the opportunity to ask her about **DUDE 3**. (I remember Amy LOVES the band.)

"Are you going to see them?" I say.

"I WISH!" she tells me. "I don't have a ticket." Then Marcus (who just can't help himself because he is a nosy twit) butts in.

"I've got V.I.P. tickets."

His dad knows someone who
knows someone who knows
someone who has got them tickets ... yawn.

I tell him V.I.P. stands for

Very Irritating
Person.

And he believes me. Ha! Ha!

So I invite Amy to the concert with me and
Derek, and my dad.
(I don't mention Uncle Kevin, Aunty Alice and
the cousins.) And she says "OK" and goes
back to reading.

"BRILLIANT," I say and that's it.

All sorted. We're all going to see my favourite band. That was easy. Then stupidly, I stop listening to the history lesson and imagine being at the concert instead (which is much more fun).

DUDE3 are fantastic - playing all their great songs. Suddenly, in the middle of a guitar solo, the **DUDE 3** guitarist is taken ill and has to be dramatically carried off stage.

The lead singer asks the crowd, *"Does anyone know how to play* **DUDE 3** *songs?"*

"ME!" I shout and jump on stage. The crowd cheers. Amy cheers. Derek cheers. I start to play and the crowd are amazed. They begin to call my name.

TOM! *TOM!*

TOM!

TOM!

TOM!

Mr Fullerman is shouting at me. (I've missed most of the history lesson.)

Worth it, though.

Will catch up tonight and get back into Mr Fullerman's good books by not being late for the school trip tomorrow.

Which I'm really looking forward to now. ☺

School Trip

Mr Fullerman is not pleased because I am LATE again. It was Delia's fault (well, that's what I tell Mr Fullerman).

Everyone is already on the coach and very excited.

Especially Norman Watson, who keeps leaping up and down in his seat.

On the coach, I can only see one spare seat left, right next to...

NO, not Mrs Worthing"tash"!

Free seat

Hello, Tom!

Derek has already saved me a place by him.
But he thinks it's funny to watch me panic.
"Your face!" he laughs.
"Ha! Ha! Very funny," I say.

The coach journey takes AGES
because some of the class need the toilet and
Julia Morton feels travel sick (she's
gone a nasty shade of green).
So we have to keep stopping.
Eventually we arrive at
the museum.

It's HUGE, with big
stone steps up to old wooden doors that
have massive pillars either side. Lots of other
schools are there (all better behaved than us).

We get split up into three groups with one teacher each (we've got Mrs Nap).

We're all given an **Egyptian Q**uiz to do. I'm in Amy's group with Derek, so we rush round the museum, mostly copying what Amy writes. The quiz doesn't take long so we get to check out the gift shop early.

I know exactly what I want to buy.

At lunchtime SOMEONE (OK, me) gives Norman half a caramel wafer. (I forget that sugar makes Norman even more hyper than usual.)

We are all sitting listening to the Museum Egyptian Expert. She is showing us a real mummy and telling us in great GORY detail how the Egyptians would

"use a long hook to pull out the dead person's brain through their nose before mummifying them..."

Julia Morton goes green and feels sick again.

Norman can't sit still and wants to take a
closer look at the mummy.

He JUMPS up a bit too quickly and

pushes Brad Galloway, who bumps into
Leroy, who falls ON SOLID, who accidentally
shoves Mrs Worthington. Then she falls
over and knocks into a very rare
Egyptian vase...

Thankfully Mr Fullerman manages to CATCH IT!

He's holding on to it really tightly and breathing a sigh of relief just when Julia Morton leans forward and is sick.

(I don't think that's what Egyptian vases were originally used for.)

The museum expert can't get rid of us quickly enough.
While Julia is getting "cleaned up" we all get to go to the gift shop again.
I buy some brilliant Egyptian tattoos.

On the way home the coach is much quieter because some kids have gone to sleep. Including Marcus. Which is excellent news because:

1. I don't have to listen/talk to him (he's annoying).
2. I'm still cross he got me kicked out of choir practice.
3. It gives me a chance to try out my new "Egyptian tattoos".

➡️

Which work a treat!

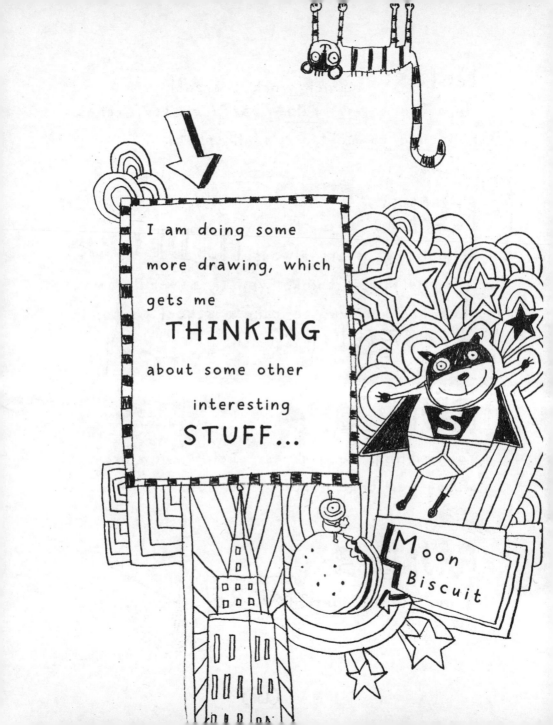

I am doing some more drawing, which gets me **THINKING** about some other interesting **STUFF...**

Moon Biscuit

Rules:

Here are a few rules based on stuff that's happened to me (so it's all true).

RULE 1.

School photos are always HIDEOUS. It's the law, I think. Even if a world-famous photographer was to take a school photo, it would STILL be rubbish.

HIDEOUS school photo

RULE 2.

Your siblings (in my case, Delia) know ways to annoy you that nobody else does.

RULE 3.

Your parents get MORE embarrassing with age.

My dad is now officially the

WORLD CHAMPION of embarrassing dads.

When we got back from the school trip, Dad
was there to pick me up.
He was wearing:
A nasty-coloured bobble hat with his name
on it.

FRANK

Muddy jeans tied up with a piece of string.

NO belt, just STRing.

A grubby shirt with holes and patches.

And filthy old wellington boots.

"I've been gardening," he said.
(Like that's an excuse!)
"Well, I won't bother to pick you up again."
(If only.)

Brad Galloway and Mark Clump both thought
he was a tramp.

Ha! Ha! Ha!

Ha!

"Look at that tramp over there," they laughed.
"Imagine if he was YOUR DAD !"
    Brad said.

Ha!

"He is my dad," I told them. I couldn't get home fast enough.

I only forgave Dad when he pulled out four (slightly muddy) tickets from his pocket.

BRILLIANT !

(<u>That</u>'s why he came to pick me up.)

I'm officially excited now and very happy.

AT home Delia spoils everything by waving my school photo around and laughing at it. "**FREAK** photo or WHAT?"

Annoyingly, I have to agree. It's AWFUL, terrible, a really rotten, cheesy picture.

HIDEOUS
school
photo

I've got odd hair and a red face. I knew it would be bad, but not *that* bad.

AGHH!

I grab it back from her and try to hide it before Mum sees it. Delia says,

"TOO LATE, **NERD BOY.**"

Apparently Mum loves it and has already ordered about a million copies for the entire family...

GROAN.

ToM'S School Photo

I tell Derek about the **DUDE3** tickets. Derek tells me he's got his <u>NEW</u> PUPPY!! He's going to bring the puppy over to mine tonight for band practice so I can see it. (Also Delia is allergic to dogs and that will keep her away.)

In Class

Mr Fullerman appears to be in a good mood. (Despite me only just making it to school on time ... *and* forgetting my review homework AGAIN.)

"Today we're going to be making models of pyramids."

(Which sounds like fun for a change.)

He puts us into groups. I'm with Norman, Amber, Pansy, Indrani and SOLID.
(I have to move tables.)
Solid has a good idea for the shape of the model.
"It should be sort of pyramid-shaped?"
GENIUS.

Indrani draws a card template and Amber cuts it out. Then we all help to cover it in glue and paper, which makes a nice and sturdy model.

Everyone is working together really well (unusually for Class 5F). Our pyramid is actually starting to look a bit like ... a pyramid.

Mr Fullerman's attention is on Mark Clump's group, who aren't doing so well.

Then Norman starts to get bored. (He gets bored easily.)

"Let's make a mummy," he suggests.

GREAT IDEA.

Norman gets six loo rolls from the school toilet and tries to "wrap up" SOLID. But there's not enough paper to cover him (too big and tall). So we use Norman instead. He's smaller but a lot more fidgety.

"Keep still, Norman," I tell him.

It's not easy covering his legs and head with the loo roll. When he's finally mummified, Norman starts walking around with his arms stretched out (like a real mummy).

He makes noises.

It's very realistic. He's good.

He's scaring Amber. **AGH!**

Mr Fullerman looks over to see what we're up to.

SUDDENLY, Mr Keen the headmaster

bursts into the classroom.

(On one of his little visits.)

Norman is still behind the door. He doesn't move.

Mr Keen asks about the school trip and admires our pyramid work.

(WHHHHOOOOOOOOOOAA WOOOOOOOOOOOOAAA)

"What's that strange moaning noise?"

The class start laughing.

(WHHHHOOOOOOOOOOAA WOOOOOOOOOOOOAAA)

"There it is again."

Mr Keen's face starts to hover around the "getting cross" colour on the Red-O-Meter when he's called away by an announcement from Mrs Mumble. And as Mr Keen closes the door, everyone can now see Norman making

WHHHHOOOOOOOOOOAA WOOOOOOOOOOOOOOAAA

noises and pretending to be a mummy.

Including Mr Fullerman.
Who's not in such a good mood now.

WHHOOOOOOOOOOAAAA
WHHOOOOOOOOOOOOAAAAA

It's been an eventful
day at school.

(Caretaker Stan replacing toilet rolls →)

I can't wait to meet Derek's new PUPPY now! He's very cute (unlike Derek), although I can see a slight similarity from the picture he emailed me.

We let him run around my house .... into Delia's room. Where he chews a few pairs of sunglasses and jumps on her bed.

GOOD DOG!

 Delia is furious.

But she has to keep her distance because she's allergic to dogs.

Derek and I are busy practising some new

DOGZOMBIES tunes (Derek's dog

is ~~singing~~ sorry, *howling* along)

OOWWl

when Dad pops his head round the door. He wants to know if we need another guitarist for the band. (We don't.)

hello!

He says things like that in a jokey kind of way. But sometimes I think he really means it. Dad reminds us about the concert next week.

Apparently Delia's not coming with us because she's going with "friends" (I think she has a boyfriend, which is a horrible thought). At least she won't be able to spoil my fun like usual.

Uncle Kevin, Aunty Alice and the twins are meeting us at the concert. I feel sorry for anyone who ends up standing behind the twins. They won't see a thing.

Can't see

DUDE3   DUDE3

Derek and I discuss wearing our DUDE3 T-shirts.
(Must check what Dad plans to wear just in case it's too embarrassing. It will be.)

TOM ...
where is your HOMEWORK?

Mr Fullerman is in a really BAD mood
today.
I keep forgetting to bring in my review
homework.
I'm going to get another detention at this
rate.
He's not pleased at all.

Plus we have parents' evening tonight
(I forgot about THAT as well).
Now Mum and Dad will be the LAST parents
to see Mr Fullerman.

Because I didn't bring my form. ☹
Being last will give them far too much time to
look at my work and "chit-chat" to everyone
(teachers and other parents - it will be
awful).

Mr Fullerman gives us today's work.

CLASS 5F

Today, I'd like you to write a piece about your HOBBIES.

Anything that you do outside of school.
Sports, music, swimming, singing.
Do you collect stamps?
Do you like drawing?
Why did you start the hobby?
What does it mean to you?
Do you need any special equipment?
Have you won any prizes?
Would you recommend this hobby to anyone else?

Write at least one A4 page, please.

Mr Fullerman

Mmmmmm ... hobbies?

My hobbies are

🙂 annoying Delia

🙂 being in a band

🙂 and eating caramel wafers.

I could write a whole A4 page on annoying Delia, but I'm not sure that's what Mr Fullerman had in mind.

What to write? What to write??

I KNOW - I'll make up a more interesting hobby for me to do. Something funny?

Good idea.

We spend most of the day sorting out our classroom and getting our books ready for parents' evening.

Marcus leaves his books out on his desk while he goes to the toilet.

(Mistake!)

I slip a few drawings I've done in between the pages of his work.

(That should make his parents' evening more interesting.)

Mr Fullerman is PIG MAN

by Marcus

My parents are thick

Ha Ha Ha!

Ha Ha

Mr Fullerman

Is an IDIOT

PARENTS' EVENING

Mum and Dad (as predicted) are not happy that they'll be the last parents to see Mr Fullerman.

It's always a bit weird coming back into school in the evening. Especially when the classroom is all clean and tidy (not like normal).
Mr Fullerman is wearing a suit and looks uncomfortable.
Dad is wearing a terrible T-shirt, so I beg him to leave his jacket on.

SHAME

Mum insists on looking at EVERY piece of work up on the walls. Worse still, she keeps talking to teachers LOVELY work! that I don't have lessons with **AND** parents of kids I don't even know. **SO** It's **SO** embarrassing!

I spot SOLID, who doesn't look happy (he looks JUST like his **DAD**, though).

"Parents' evening sucks," he whispers.

I agree.

Then I see Amy. Her parents are with Mr Fullerman already. They are both smiling and laughing (no problems with Amy's work, then).

Dad says he's got Amy's DUDE3 tickets in his pocket DUDE3 and he could give it to her "folks" now.

(Folks? Don't say folks, please?)

So we wait for them to finish. Then Dad strikes up a conversation with Amy's dad about MUSIC in a really LOUD voice.

Amy rolls hers eyes and looks at me. "Sorry," I say, and we both have to stand there and wait for our parents to stop embarrassing us. They chat for ages about all kinds of rubbish.

Then Dad forgets to give them the tickets after all that!

Finally, when **M**r Fullerman has seen all the other parents, it's our turn ... groan.

He brings out a folder that's full of letters.

← Tom's letters

"Can I start with Tom's letters from home?" he says.

Mum and Dad look a bit puzzled.

Not the LETTERs NO!!

(I've been rumbled.)

Dear Mr Fullerman

Poor Tom has a cold and can't do sports outside ... ever.

Love from

Rita Gates

Dear Mr Fullerman

Please can Tom be excused from Spelling this week. He's had a difficult week (family stuff).

Thanks

Rita Gates

Dear Mr Fullerman

Tom has been helping his sick grandmother and has not been able to do his homework.

Sorry

Rita Gates

Dear Mr Fullerman

Tom's delayed homework was due to his
sister being nasty to him and not
letting him use the computer. We have
told her off.

Thanks

Frank Gates

Dear Mr Fullerman

Tom has been helping his sick
grandfather and has not been able to
do his homework.

Whoops

Frank Gates

Dear Mr Fullerman

Please can Tom be excused from
swimming?
He is allergic to ~~water~~ chemicals in
the water.

Thank you

Rita Gates

It's not a good start to parents' evening.
(What can I say? ... It worked for a while.)

But the good news is, I'm doing well at ART
and English.

Spelling is only so-so. Could improve at maths.
Could do better at science and history. Good
at PE.

It's not all bad.
Room for improvement, Mr Fullerman says.

They have a nice chat about me (like I'm not
there).

I smile and agree not to:

1. ☺ Chat so much. ☺

2. so much.

3. ☺ Fake letters from home again.

Generally I'm an OK kid.

It's a *reasonably* good parents' evening.
Then Mum and Dad both read

"MY NEW HOBBY" (which I completely
forgot about). And it all goes HORRIBLY
wrong.
From the looks on their faces I can see
they're not happy.

MY NEW HOBBY

By Tom Gates

My mum and dad like to use my pocket money as an extra way of making me do things I'm not very keen on doing.

For instance...
"Tidy your room ... or no pocket money."
"Eat your vegetables ... or no pocket money."
"Be nice to your sister ... or no pocket money."
(Which I think is possibly against my human rights?) And if that's not bad enough, Dad seems to take great pleasure in placing my money on very high places. Like doors, shelves, and anywhere I can't easily reach it.

When I do finally get my hands on it, **M**um often borrows it back to buy milk and newspapers. Emergency money is what she says.

I discovered my new hobby completely by accident.

Fed up of listening to Mum and Mrs Fingle (Derek's mum) "chit-chatting" outside the shops (for what seems like HOURS), I sit on the pavement and look really Chit-chatting bored (my legs ache too). When someone walks past me, he drops some money into my lap.

Mrs Fingle

Real money!

It's **BRILLIANT!**

(I think they must feel SORRY for me?)

So I put on an even *sadder* face, and someone else gives me another £1.

By the time Mum and Mrs Fingle have finished talking, I've made £3.70 all on my own.

Which gets me thinking. What if I use a

SHAKILY written sign like

PLEASE HELP ME

and wear some old worn-out clothes?

So I give that a go too, and sure enough I make even MORE money.

The great thing about my new hobby is you can do it anywhere and you get to meet

LOTS of different people. And now I don't have to rely on Mum and Dad for my pocket money any more. It's a hobby I would recommend to **EVERYONE**.

I am also in a band called

But we don't make any money at all (yet).

The End

"YOU'VE BEEN BEGGING?

I CAN'T BELIEVE IT!"

BEGGING!

Mum and Dad keep looking ⊙ ⊙ at me and
shaking their heads.

(I wasn't begging; it's just a STORY.)

On the way home, they remind me again that
NOT everyone is as lucky as you, Tom."

And "begging is no joke!"

I'm trying to convince them that I was
not begging. I tell them I was using my
imagination.

I would NEVER beg. EVER!

"It was just a story! You know, pretending ...
ha ha ha?"

I think they believe me now. Phew.

Delia hears Mum and Dad talking about my parents' evening and how they thought I'd been begging.
She suddenly comes over and offers me a caramel wafer. Even though I KNOW she's up to something, I STUPIDLY go to take it.

"I hear you're good at begging? Beg for the wafer, then," she says, and wafts the wafer in front of me. I want that wafer SO badly that I actually say "PLEASE."
And she says, "SAY PRETTY PLEASE."
So I say, "PRETTY PLEASE."

(It's so humiliating.)

"I can't hear you!"

"PRETTY PLEASE!"

Then, to my surprise, Delia actually hands over the wafer and goes off laughing.

It's only when I try and open the wafer I realize that I have fallen for the old "empty biscuit wrapper" trick.

Very funny, Delia.

Very funny.

I suddenly feel inspired to write a new song. When Derek comes round later I show him a new song I've just written for

DOG ZOMBIES

He likes it a LOT!

Delia's a Weirdo

Who's that weirdo over there?
Dressed in **black**
With greasy hair
You can't trust her
She's not nice
She's got no heart ✗
Just a block of ice

CHORUS   Delia
             She's a WEIRDO
             Delia
             She's a GEEK
             Delia
             She's a WEIRDO
             Delia
             She's a FREAK

Delia's a grumpy moo
Don't let her
Stand next to you
Big black glasses
Hide her eyes
She really smells
And that's no lie

CHORUS

Tom, I'm still waiting for your HOMEWORK.

(I got carried away practising "Delia's a Weirdo". It's sounding really good. I have written a few more good verses. Will have to do homework TONIGHT ☾ *

before the **DUDE3** concert.)

I'm SO excited I can hardly concentrate.

Marcus is going on and on and ON about his V.I.P. tickets. v.i.p. v.i.p. v.i.p. v.i.p.
"Shut up, Marcus." Even Amy is fed up with him.
Mr Fullerman reminds us that **DUDE3** is not the only concert coming up (how did he know about **DUDE3**?).

"Don't forget about the SCHOOL CONCERT," he tells us.

When Mr Fullerman starts the lesson, I'm trying to work out how many hours it will be before the concert starts.

LOADS ... too many.

The clock in the classroom doesn't seem to be moving at all.
This is the LONGEST lesson Mr Fullerman has ever given us.

I am staring ⊙⊙ at the clock and it's definitely NOT moving.

The more I stare ⊙ ⊙ ... the slower the time goes.

And Mrs Mumble keeps interrupting the lesson with announcements that no one can understand.

Hello can I Please come to the office. Mr Fullerman.

Thank you!

"Did anyone understand that?" Mr Fullerman asks. Then she says it again, but it's no clearer. (This lesson is NEVER going to end!)

Mr Fullerman leaves the classroom to check what's going on. **"It might be important,"** he says. (As if.)
While he's gone, I have a

BRAINWAVE!

I stand on the table and MOVE the hands on the clock **forward** so the lesson is nearly finished. (This goes down well with my classmates.)

Hooray Hooray! **HOORAY!**

Mr Fullerman looks slightly confused when he comes back. He checks his own watch. **"Is the clock fast?"**

"NO, MR FULLERMAN."

"Has anyone touched the clock?"

"NO, MR FULLERMAN."

He notices the clock is slightly wonky on the wall. Mr Fullerman is not convinced. He stands on a chair to put the clock back to the right time.

Just as Mrs Mumble makes another anouncement. It makes Mr Fullerman jump, and he wobbles off the chair and on to the floor.

It's a DISASTER!

(**W**e'll **never** get out of this lesson at this rate.)
Not that I'm being unsympathetic. But this is turning out to be the longest lesson EVER.

Mr Fullerman is wincing in pain and takes TWICE as long to do or say anything. And the rest of the day doesn't go any faster.
(It's like someone knows it's the concert tonight and is deliberately slowing the world down.)

MATHS is a drag. PE takes for ever.
I'm getting changed out of my PE kit in the sports changing rooms when there is another really loud noise that starts

BLARING

out of the speakers.

(Not Mrs Mumble this time.
Something even LOUDER.)

Mr Fullerman says it's a

FIRE ALarm DRILL!

"Leave everything and exit in an orderly fashion. DON'T RUN! Go outside."

I manage to grab my shoes and follow everyone else outside to the playground. Even though we have to **wait** for the register to be taken and wait for all the other classes to come out. Time suddenly seems to be *FLYING* by. Mainly because Marcus has left his trousers behind and is standing in the playground in just his pants.

Mrs Nap gives him a jumper to tie round his waist. Now it looks like he's wearing a skirt.

It's the FUNNIEST thing I've seen in ages.

Mr Fullerman says we can all go home
slightly early now. HOORAY!

Shame!

I'm telling Derek all about
what happened to Marcus on
the way home (especially the
jumper/skirt bit), when he
tells me he's got a proper
name for his dog now.
I try to guess what it is.
"Rocky?"
"Rover?"
"Fang?"
"It's ROOSTER," he says.
"ROOSTER? That's a kind of chicken, isn't it?
You're naming your dog after a chicken?"
(I suppose I'll get used to it.)

DUDE3 HERE WE COME!

CLUCK

DUDE 3 CONCERT

Derek has brought Rooster over and he's running around our house looking for Delia. She's already gone to meet her friend (boyfriend, more like). Derek and I are wearing our DUDE 3 T-shirts and looking cool.

Dad is wearing another terrible T-shirt and horrid trousers. He <u>doesn't</u> look cool.

Mum agrees with me and makes him change. "And no crowd surfing," she tells Dad as we leave the house.

Change.

Then DAD remembers the tickets were in his other trousers. So he goes back to get them. But he can't find them **ANYWHERE**.

THIS IS DREADFUL.

Don't panic.

I PANIC!

Derek is trying not to panic.
We look round the whole house. In Delia's room, my room, the kitchen.
"Don't worry, they're here somewhere," he says. He checks his pockets. The bedrooms, the bathroom. We are officially FRANTIC.
Where are the tickets?

YAP! YAP! YAP! YAP! YAP!

Rooster is running around chasing us from room to room. It's really annoying because he is barking and yapping and it's making everyone stressed.

Mum sends Rooster out to the garden.
I'm checking my room again when I look out
of the window and see Rooster playing with
some bits of paper. The bits of paper look like
they could have been...

THE TICKETS!

"BAD ROOSTER!" Derek is saying. But
it's too late. The tickets are all mangled and
covered in teeth marks and dog drool.

"I'll stick them together," Dad says. "It'll be
fine."
But it's not fine. The tickets are   ruined .

"**M**aybe Uncle Kevin and Aunty Alice will sell us their tickets?" Dad says.

"Don't bank on it," Mum says.

"We'll think of something," Dad says.

But I'm too STUNNED to say anything at all.

We go to the gig anyway.

"I'm never going to get a dog," I say to Derek. Which is a bit unfair, I know, because it's not his fault. I'm just really angry with his stupid chicken dog. GGGGGGGGGGGrrrrrrrrrrrrrr.

BAD Rooster →

Amy is already there waiting with her dad. "Let's see if they'll take the tickets anyway?" says Dad. The man on the door takes one look at the bits of ticket and shakes his head.

"Sorry, mate. Can't take these, they're all mashed up."

Just when things couldn't get any worse ... Marcus and his dad turn up clutching four V.I.P. tickets. Turns out that they now have two spare V.I.P. tickets. And Marcus's dad suggests that we could have them. (Marcus doesn't take after his dad, who seems quite nice.)

Marcus's Dad →

V.I.P. Tickets ←

I want to go SO badly. But my DAD says that Amy and Derek should go. "Because we might be able to get in with Uncle Kevin."
I am VERY ⊙ ⊙ brave. I tell Amy and Derek that I really don't mind and that I'll be fine. Then I watch all four of them go off to the concert. (Inside I can't believe Derek and

Amy have gone with **MARCUS!)**

This is terrible.

Uncle Kevin and **A**unty **A**lice are waving and calling Dad. Uncle Kevin is looking particularly pleased with himself. Dad tells him what's happened and how we can't get in now with the mangled tickets. Uncle Kevin says, (TYPICAL YOU!) which makes Dad cross. Uncle Kevin (being a salesman) has actually sold their tickets for three times as much as he paid for them. He's very happy and they're going for dinner instead of the concert. (I think the cousins would rather have seen the band.)

Great, this is turning into a nightmare.
I'll NEVER get to see my favourite band
now.
Dad sees I'm **REALLY** upset.

"Stay here, don't move," he says. "I'll get
some tickets, don't you worry, Tom."

I'm SO miserable.

I sit on the floor and look
really fed up. The concert
is about to start and we've
got no chance of seeing them at this rate.

Then I have an idea.
It's a long shot, but I've got NOTHING to
lose.

I'm desperate.

I find a paper bag and I
already have a pen.

Then I get writing and
drawing.

I'm attracting a bit of attention, but no tickets as yet.

A lady walks past and says "Poor you," which is nice.

Then I'm suddenly aware of a man in leather trousers reading my note.
He's shaking his head and looking at me.

I put on an extra SAD face.

Then he starts walking towards me and there's something very familiar about him.
I'm sure I've seen him before.
Then he asks me a question.

"Is this your new hobby, Tom?"
he asks, and it SUDDENLY dawns on me who it is...

BLIMEY, iT'S MR FULLERMAN.

AGH! →

LEATHER TROUSERS!

AND he's wearing leather trousers! What's **HE** doing here? It's a terrible moment bumping into a TEACHER outside of school. You don't really think of them having a life outside of being a teacher.

It's a shock (especially the leather trousers).

Dad comes back, with no tickets.
He's NOT pleased to see me begging.

YOU'RE BEGGING?

"You told me it was a made-up story, Tom!"
"It was ... I was desperate!" I say.
"Stop begging right now! There must be
another way to see DUDE3 ."

Then Mr Fullerman says,
**"Hello, Mr Gates. I think I might be
able to help."**

And Dad looks as shocked as me
to see it's Mr Fullerman (wearing
leather trousers).
I'm wondering what Mr Fullerman is doing at
a DUDE3 gig in the first place. And guess
what?

Turns out that Mr Fullerman actually went to school MATES with DUDE 3's MANAGER!

They are good friends.

(Mr Fullerman is NOT just a crusty old teacher after all.)

Thanks, man   No problem, nice trousers

He speaks to someone backstage who gives us all special passes.

SQUEAK!

NOW I can watch the whole gig from the side of the stage!

I would HUG Mr Fullerman if he wasn't my teacher (and wearing leather trousers).

It's the BEST view ever!

are absolutely brilliant and I can see **EVERYTHING**.

I see Derek and Amy and wave. Derek and Amy wave back. Marcus has his mouth open like a goldfish in shock.

(It's almost the best part of the gig. Ha ha!)

Then I spot Delia in the audience. She's with her boyfriend. So I point him out to Dad and stir things up by saying he's got a VERY bad reputation around town.

What a fantastic night I'm having. DUDE3 play all their best songs.
Then right at the end ... it gets better...

(I'll never wash again.)

I'm still buzzing when I get home.

Dad has forgotten about my begging note
(phew).

He's too busy worrying about Delia's dodgy
boyfriend.

I go to bed **happy** and relive the
whole gig in my head.

This is probably the

In the morning, Delia is slopping around the house sulking and being miserable. **Grrrrrrrr**

Apparently it's all my fault because Mum and Dad want to meet her new "friend" now. (I am a GENIUS.)

Dad is humming DUDE3 songs at breakfast. mmmmmmmmmmm

 Mum is wearing a DUDE3 T-shirt.

It's SO embarrassing (old people trying to be trendy). I can't get out of the house quick enough.
Derek and I go to school together.

He's SO wishing he'd stuck with me at the concert now.

Seeing Mr Fullerman again in "teacher" mode is REALLY weird.

The first thing he asks me is,

"WHERE'S YOUR HOMEWORK, TOM?"

"I was at the concert, sir, remember?"

Mr Fullerman says that's no excuse and I'll get a detention unless I bring it in first thing in the morning, which is a bit harsh?

(He's SO back in teacher mode.)

With all the excitement about DUDE3, I completely forget about the school concert, which apparently is

TODAY.

I'm not worried because I'm not in it.

(No choir, which is a relief.) Phew.

Mrs Nap is looking for helpers to put chairs out in the hall.

Helpers get to miss lessons, so I volunteer.

All I have to do is show the little kids what to do. HOW hard is that?

We get all the chairs out when they start to mess around. I get TOUGH and suggest a quick game of musical ♩ ♪ chairs, which keeps them happy. There's no music - so I sing my DOGZOMBIES song

"Delia's a Weirdo".

It's all going VERY well. The little kids all join in and sing along with me.

"Delia, she's a weirdo!

Delia, she's a freak!" (Very catchy chorus.)

Then I sing the verse...

When Mr Keen pops his head round the door
to see how we're doing.
We all pretend to be arranging the chairs.
(Little kids learn fast.)

"That's a jolly song, Tom," he says.

"Really, Mr Keen?"

"Are you performing in the concert today?"

"No, Mr Keen."

"Why not? You should be! I'll have a word with Mrs Nap to give you a slot at the end."

"No, Mr Keen, it's fine... Really, I don't want to sing."

"Nonsense, that sounded excellent. Don't you agree, children?"

And all the little kids cheer and say,

"YES!"

Groan ... that's ALL I need.

This could be very humiliating.
CORRECTION. It WILL be very humiliating.

Fool

I don't think Mr Keen heard all the lyrics to the song, either.

"ARE YOU MAD?

Of course I DON'T want to play in the school concert!" Derek says.

NO WAY!

He thinks **DOG ZOMBIES** have to plan their first gig very carefully.

(In other words, we're still a bit rubbish and need more practice.)

BUT he does come up with a BRILLIANT plan that will get me off the hook and save me from serious humiliation. ☺

The **ONLY** good thing about the school concert is we get to go home early to "prepare". (Eat caramel wafers, in my case.)

Mum says, "What do you mean there's a school concert tonight?"

(I forgot to tell them.)

"And you're in it?"

"Sort of..." I say.

Mum and Dad planned to meet Delia's dodgy "boyfriend" tonight.

"I'm not leaving them here on their own," Dad says. "They'll both have to come to the concert too."

Ha Ha! Delia will be delighted!

A romantic night out ... at my school concert.

She'll be so cross it's almost worth being in the concert for.

Derek and I run through our plan one last time on the way back to school.

It has to work or I'll be stuffed.

Back at school, the hall is already packed with people. Mum and Dad sit at the back, which is a relief because Mum has on her DUDE3 T-shirt and Dad is wearing gardening gear. ← Patches

Delia and her "boyfriend" look jolly (NOT).

Derek and I run through our plan one last time (I hope it works).

The lights go down and the concert begins.
First, there's some (slightly boring) poetry.

The star was bright.
We got a big fright.
That night.

Then we have to sit through some songs
and of course the choir.
Watching Marcus and
Solid SWAYING from side
to side is hilarious.

Amy is very good (of course).

swaying

AMY

There's a play by Year
Three. (Quite funny.)
And a dance by Year Six.

(It's rubbish.)

Then Mr Keen makes a speech about what a
good term it's been
blah blah blah.
And I hear him telling EVERYONE how he heard
me singing and thought I should be in the
concert.

It's AWFUL ... I can feel myself getting
nervous and sweaty.

Now it's my turn.
Mr Keen asks me what my song is called.

"Delia's a Weirdo'," I say.

Which makes everyone laugh ... apart from
Delia, who's giving me the EVILS.

I sit on the stage and clear my throat.
Everyone is looking at me and waiting.

So I clear my throat again ...

and wait ...
and wait ...

and strum a little (like I'm warming up).
(Mr Keen is glaring at me now.)
So I'm thinking I might have to actually
start singing if Derek's plan doesn't work...

When at long LAST...

A VERY Loud BLARING NOiSE goes OFF

Mr Fullerman tells everyone not to panic.
It's just the

FIRE ALARM!

We all have to leave the
hall straightaway.

The concert is abandoned.

RESULT!

Derek is a **GENIUS!** He gives me a THUMBS UP as we leave school.

Better still ... Delia can hear some little children singing my song...

DELIA She's a weirdo DELIA She's a FREAK!

She's not happy but her boyfriend is laughing ... he won't be her boyfriend for long at this rate!

What's funny!

Mum and Dad think it's a shame I didn't get to do my song. (I don't!)

"Maybe next time, don't write about your sister, though," Mum tells me. "It only upsets her." (EXACTLY!)

Dad suggests writing about someone else who annoys me instead.

"Like Uncle Kevin," he adds. Which makes me laugh.

But Mum is giving him the EVILS now.
(Uh-oh!)

When we get home, Dad and I escape to his shed to eat his secret stash of caramel wafers. (TREAT!)

It's the last day of term tomorrow. So I MUSN'T FORGET.

I only have tonight to finish my review homework. (It's the last piece I have left to do.)

I know, I'll review the school concert.
That won't take long!
Just eat the last wafer biscuit and wrap it up for Delia first... Ha ha!
And draw a few more pictures.

THEN I'll start my homework...

.......in the morning.

(I'll have **LOADS** of time
to do it if I get up early tomorrow.)

This is a good idea

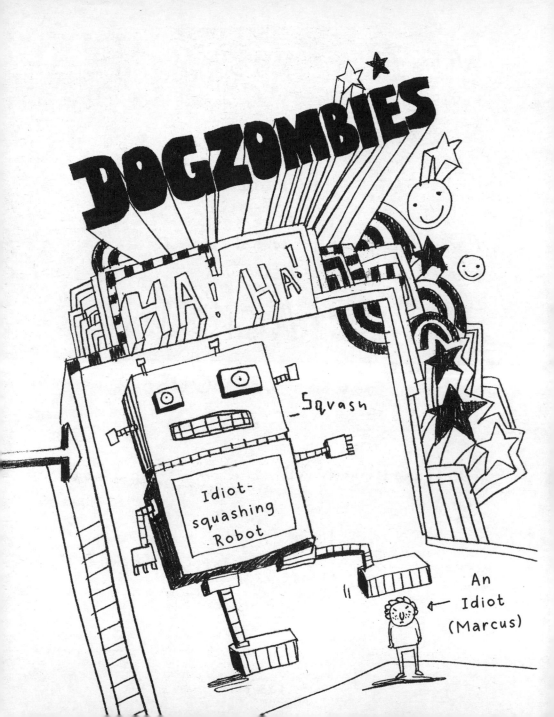

Mr Fullerman, I'm SO sorry about my REVIEW homework.

As you can see I DID do it.

Let me explain.

I was on my way to school when I was followed and

AttACkED

by a VICIOUS dog.

I defended myself with the only thing I could think of.

My exercise book.

LUCKILY I survived (just).
But my REVIEW HOMEWORK didn't...

Sorry again...

Oh dear, Tom.
I was looking forward to finally
reading it.
You will just have do it again over
the holidays.
In the meantime let's hope you don't
get abducted by aliens
or attacked by GIANTS.
What an eventful life you have.
See you (and your homework) next
term.

Mr Fullerman

(Result!) ☺

Dog drool →

My Review
By Tom Gates

Vicious teeth marks ↗ ↘ ↓

← More dog drool

The End

Turn over for something nicer

How to draw my grumpy sister Delia

1. ← Draw this shape.

2. ← Then her glasses...

3. ← Colour them in.

4. Ears ... (even though she doesn't LISTEN).

Add her manky hair ...

5. ... and add a gloom cloud...

Keep your BEADY EYES open for the other hilarious TOM GATES books!

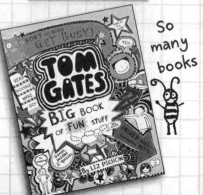

So many books

Liz Pichon is one of the UK's best-loved and bestselling creators of children's books.

Her TOM GATES series has been translated into 45 languages, sold millions of copies worldwide, and has won the Roald Dahl Funny Prize, the Blue Peter Book Award for Best Story and the younger fiction category of the Waterstones Children's Book Prize.

In the ten years since THE BRILLIANT WORLD OF TOM GATES first published, the books have inspired the nation's children to get creative, whether that's through reading, drawing, doodling, writing, making, music or performing.

"I wanted to FILL the books with ALL the things I loved doing when I was a kid. It's just the best feeling ever to know children are enjoying reading the books, because I love making them. So thank you so much for choosing Tom Gates and keep reading and doodling!"

ONE VILE VILLAIN.
TWO VICIOUS DOGS.
THREE COURAGEOUS CHILDREN.

The flying shoes of your most EPIC dreams.

WELCOME TO SHOE TOWN.

Meet Ruby, Bear and Chelsea. They're RUNNING out of time to RESCUE their inventor dad from his HIDEOUS boss, WENDY WEDGE.

She'll do anything to win the glitzy GOLDEN SHOE AWARD and knows that entering flying shoes is her hot ticket to the trophy. Flying shoes that Ruby and Bear just HAPPEN to be hiding…

This can only mean one thing… it's SHOE WARS!

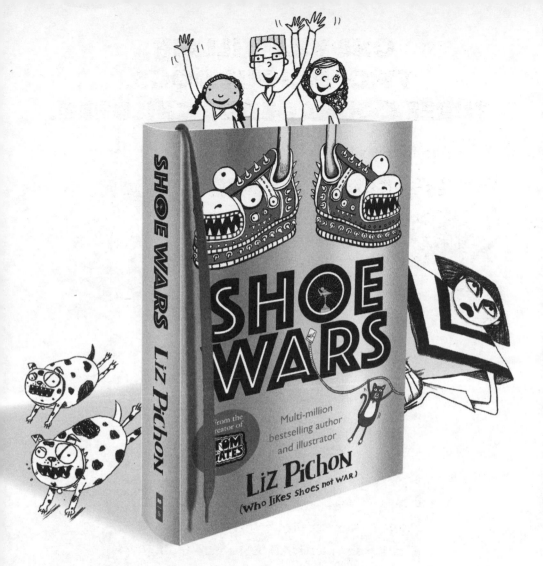

A laugh-out-loud, gadget-packed,
wedge-of-your-feet adventure like no other!

A *Sunday Times* children's book of the year.

"Full of Pichon's characteristic warmth, humour
and quirky illustrations" *The Bookseller*

Thank you all so much if you took part in the doodle competition. It was so hard to choose a winner – they were all brilliant. WELL DONE!

10 YEARS

The WINNER!

TOM GATES

Delia's Sunglasses

Mum spying on New Neighbour

water

Caramel wafer (yum)

Amy and Florence

bote 3

Derek my mate

Brill my mate

Daisy, 8, Peterborough

Runners Up

Ava, 9, London

Oscar, 8, Todmorden

Laila, 14, London

Theo, 8, Gloucestershire

Josie, 8, Penarth

Stasha, 10, India

Ayaan, 9, Bromley

Ayaan, 9, Bromley

Emilia, 6, London

Iyla, 7, Eastbourne

Alexa, 10, Loughborough

Euan, 11, Stockport

River, 10, Falmouth

Annalie, 10, Woking

Lilly, 8, Eastbourne

Cayden, 11, Ferndale, Rhondda Cynon Taf

Ben, 10, Southampton

Jess, 12, Derbyshire

Inari, 13, Surrey

Wren, 6, Lancaster

Sebastian, 8, Telford

Isla, 9, Silverstone

Thomas, 8, Liverpool

Luca, 8, Eastbourne

Aurora, 10, Surrey

Camille, 9, Kent

Luca, 8, Eastbourne

Annie, 7, Shropshire

Sidra, 11, London

Harrison, 6, Hertfordshire

Joshua, 9, Middlesbrough

Evie, 12, Stockport

Oenone, 12, Bedfordshire

Ralph, 8, Chichester

Joseph, 9, Stockport

Zackaria, 8, Edinburgh

Ruari, 10, London

Joseph, 9, Tonbridge

Leo, 7, Bristol

Oliver, 7, Shoreham by Sea

Amira, 13, London

Stanley, 10, Leigh on Sea

Maya, 10, Grayshott

Jennifer, 12, Lincolnshire

Oscar, 9, Eastbourne

Joseph, 11, Balfron

Hammam, 11, Sale

Sara, 11, London

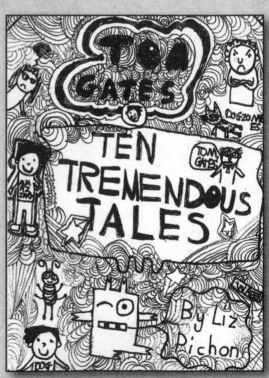

Lana, 9, London